Floppy wanted a new basket.

1

Mum and Biff went to the market.

They got a new basket.

Mum and Biff went to
the toilet.

4

"Stay Floppy," said Biff.

Floppy saw a cat.

He chased it.

The cat jumped over the oranges.

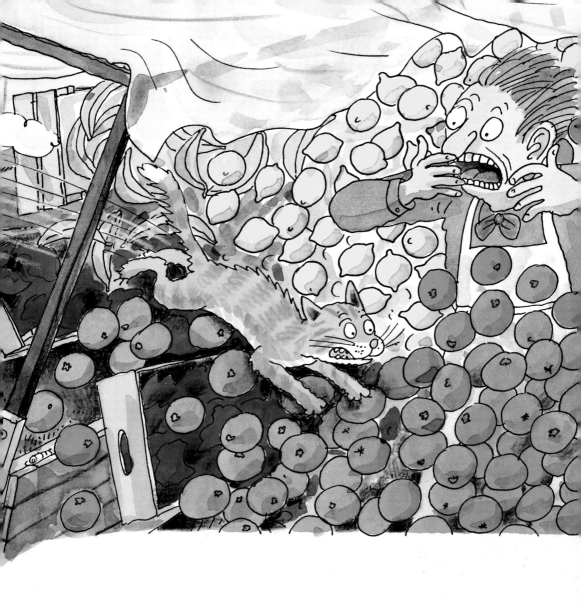

Crash went the oranges.

The cat jumped over some plates.

10

Crash went the plates.

The cat jumped over some
clothes.

"Got you!" said a man.

Everyone was cross.

"What a bad dog!"
everyone said.

"What a good dog!" said Mum.

PEACE
AT LAST

Jill Murphy

M
MACMILLAN CHILDREN'S BOOKS

For
Daniel
Celia and
Min

© Jill Murphy 1980

Published by Macmillan Children's Books
A division of Pan Macmillan Limited
London and Basingstoke
Associated companies throughout the world

ISBN 0 333 34185 6

Picturemac edition published 1982

10   9   8   7

Printed in Belgium by
Proost International Book Production

The hour was late.

Mr. Bear was tired,
Mrs. Bear was tired
and
Baby Bear was tired,
 so they all went to bed.

Mrs. Bear fell asleep.

Mr. Bear didn't.

Mrs. Bear began to snore.
"SNORE," went Mrs. Bear,
"SNORE, SNORE, SNORE."
"Oh NO!" said Mr. Bear,
"I can't stand THIS."
So he got up and went to
sleep in Baby Bear's room.

Baby Bear was not asleep either.
He was lying in bed pretending
to be an aeroplane.
"NYAAOW!" went Baby Bear,
"NYAAOW! NYAAOW!"
"Oh NO!" said Mr. Bear,
"I can't stand THIS."
So he got up
and went to sleep in the living-room.

TICK-TOCK . . . went the living-room
clock. . . .TICK-TOCK, TICK-TOCK.
CUCKOO! CUCKOO!
"Oh NO!" said Mr. Bear,
"I can't stand THIS."
So he went off to sleep in the kitchen.

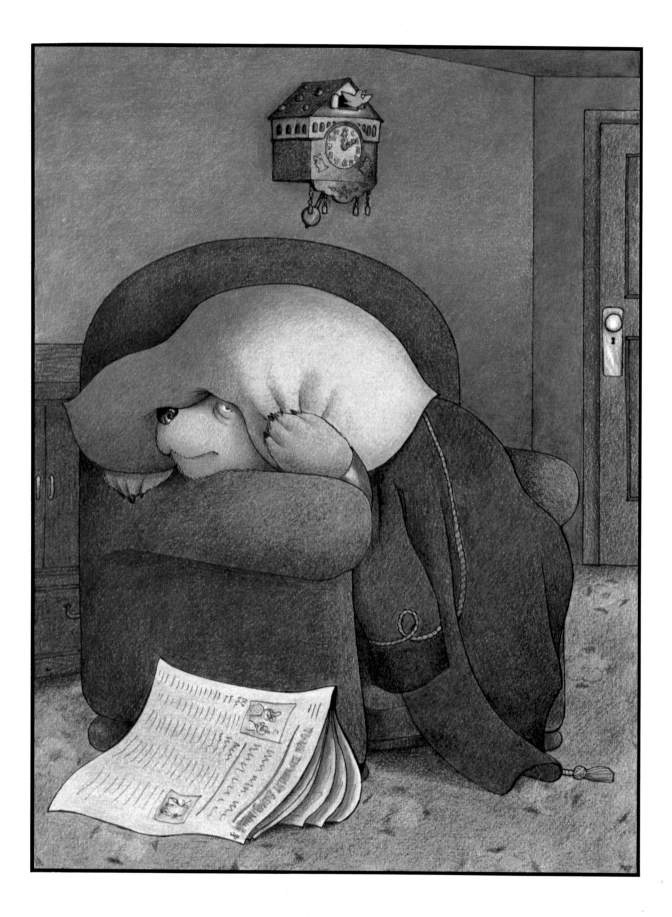

DRIP, DRIP . . . went the leaky
kitchen tap.
HMMMMMMMMMM . . .
went the refrigerator.
"Oh NO," said Mr. Bear,
"I can't stand THIS."
So he got up
and went to sleep in the garden.

Well, you would not believe
what noises there are in
the garden at night.
"TOO-WHIT-TOO-WHOO!"
went the owl.
"SNUFFLE, SNUFFLE," went
the hedgehog.
"MIAAAOW!" sang the cats
on the wall.
"Oh, NO!" said Mr. Bear,
"I can't stand THIS."
So he went off to sleep in
the car.

It was cold in the car
and uncomfortable, but
Mr. Bear was so tired
that he didn't notice.
He was just falling asleep
when all the birds started to
sing and the sun peeped in at
the window.
"TWEET TWEET!" went the birds.
SHINE, SHINE . . . went the sun.
"Oh NO!" said Mr. Bear,
"I can't stand THIS."
So he got up and went back
into the house.

In the house, Baby Bear was
fast asleep, and Mrs. Bear had
turned over and wasn't snoring
any more.
Mr. Bear got into bed and closed his
eyes.
"Peace at last," he said to himself.

BRRRRRRRRRRRRRRRR! went the
alarm-clock, BRRRRRR!
Mrs. Bear sat up and rubbed her eyes.
"Good morning, dear," she said.
"Did you sleep well?"
"Not VERY well, dear," yawned
Mr. Bear.
"Never mind," said Mrs. Bear. "I'll
bring you a nice cup of tea."

And she did.

Also available by Jill Murphy in Picturemac

WHATEVER NEXT!
ON THE WAY HOME

Other Picturemacs you will enjoy

HURRY UP, FRANKLIN Paulette Bourgeois/Brenda Clark
FRANKLIN IN THE DARK Paulette Bourgeois/Brenda Clark
WHY CAN'T I FLY? Ken Brown
ONE BEAR ALL ALONE Caroline Bucknall
ONE BEAR IN THE PICTURE Caroline Bucknall
MOUSE MISCHIEF Margaret Greaves/Jane Pinkney
A PORCUPINE NAMED FLUFFY Helen Lester/Lynn Munsinger
FARM COUNTING BOOK Jane Miller
FARM ALPHABET BOOK Jane Miller
CAN HIPPO JUMP? Gerald Rose
'AHH!' SAID STORK Gerald Rose
PENELOPE AND THE PIRATES James Young

For a complete list of Picturemac titles write to

Pan Macmillan Children's Books, 18–21 Cavaye Place,
London SW10 9PG